For Lachie, Livie,
Theo and Willow who make
the world a better place
simply by being in it

THIS BOOK BELONGS TO:

_____

GARBAGE GUTS

EMILY S. SMITH   HEIDI COOPER SMITH

In the North Pacific Ocean
lives a monster made of trash,

A hungry, greedy meanie
with a handlebar moustache.

And though his name is Garbage Guts,
he's often called Big G.

He blobs about destroying
all the oceans and the seas.

Big G, one day, was blobbing by
and munching on a nappy,

When dolphins gently splashed him,
which made him most unhappy.

'Those horrid, hateful creatures!
I detest them all,' he cried,
'I'm better than the lot of them,'
he said with spiteful pride.

'I'm sharper than a swordfish,
I'm tougher than a clam,
And as for dopey dolphins?
I'm much smarter, yes I am!'

And then he hissed with malice,
'I will make them go away',
He then devised a dreadful plan—
a "Bon Voyage" soiree.

Garbage Guts'
Great Goodbye Gathering

The party to end all parties.

Where: Garbage Guts' home,
North Pacific Ocean

When: Saturday 31st December

Time: 5pm (til everyone has gone)

At last the party night arrived,
and everyone was there,
The creatures all were overwhelmed
by Big G's grand affair.

And as the party hit full swing,
that monster said with glee,

'Soon I'll be the only thing
left living in the sea!'

That vile and wicked monster
carried out his evil scheme,
'For entrée I've made "jellyfish",
a green sea turtle's dream.

For all you fish, a side of soup'
(containing plastic pips),
And to the whales he said, 'Try these!'
Just packets without chips!

But there was more to Big G's plan,
he hadn't finished yet,
He said, 'Let's play a dress-up game
with this discarded net.'

And then he watched with sheer delight
as chaos reigned on down,

Some sea life sick from rubbish,
while the others feared they'd drown.

But then a roaring, rumbling sound
made Big G feel quite grim,
A monster, blocking out the sun,
was headed right for him!

This terrifying creature
then began to suck and slurp,
It gobbled up old Garbage Guts,
then bubbled out a...

BURP

Deep inside its belly,
was a menacing machine,
With shredders, claws and furnaces,
a horrifying scene.

Poor Garbage Guts was panic-struck,
his body shook with fear,

As two big hulking metal claws
began to draw quite near.

'It's all my fault!' Big G exclaimed,
ashamed and sorry too,

As he was dragged and dropped
between the blades that chomp and chew.

It took some time for Garbage Guts
to open up his eyes,

And what he saw before him
made him gasp with great surprise.

No longer a trash monster,
but a million different things,

Like kitty litter, yoga mats,
and seats for children's swings.

His spirit bubbled up with joy
(and fizzy cola too),

He felt relieved his wicked scheme
had quickly fallen through.

I'll educate the humans
not to let the monsters win.
I'll teach them to recycle...,